Our book pays homage to tradesmen and skilled workers all over the world. Yes, we need scientists, engineers, architects, designers, artists, and even writers and illustrators. But we want to give thanks to the women and men who work tirelessly to see our dreams brought to life.

**For my husband, Glen, jack-of-all-trades.
I'm glad we've built our dreams together. —LW**

For Virgil —LL

Dial Books for Young Readers
An imprint of Penguin Random House LLC, New York

First published in the United States of America by Dial Books for Young Readers,
an imprint of Penguin Random House LLC, 2021

Text copyright © 2021 by Lisa Wheeler
Illustrations copyright © 2021 by Loren Long

Visit us online at penguinrandomhouse.com.

Library of Congress Cataloging-in-Publication Data is available.

Printed in the United States of America • ISBN 9781984814333

10 9 8 7 6 5 4 3 2 1

Design by Lily Malcom • Text set in Verlag

The art for this book was created by hand on illustration board using acrylics, colored pencils,
and whatever dust and dog hair happened to be floating around the studio.

SOMEONE BUILDS THE DREAM

written by **Lisa Wheeler**   illustrated by **Loren Long**

Dial Books for Young Readers

All across this great big world
jobs are getting done

by many hands in many lands.
It takes much more than one.

An architect creates a space.
She'll draw, re-draw, measure, and trace—
a woodsy, warm, and peaceful place.

But . . .

Someone works to guide the saws,

plane the logs, lead the team.

Someone needs to pound the nails.
Someone has to *build* the dream.

To engineer a bridge takes skill.
Math and science fit the bill,
and I-beams ordered from the mill.

But . . .

Tension and Compr...
compression
tension

triangles △   arches

Connecto- plates
Symmetry!!!

steel beams
IRON

ARCH Bridge Roman/Baroque
                    Renaissance
—— deck

$286 \times (1+6+12)$
286×19
$C = pd = 3.14 \times 15$
$D = 15.75i$

BEAM / TRUSS Bridges ✓
GIRDER

Through truss

Deck truss
$CaCO_3$

800 ft
244 meters

62000 7,000 feet

John Roebling
Suspension Bridge

cable tension

tower compression

Torsion
Shear

Someone works to mine the ore,
smelt the iron,

pour the beam.

Someone needs to weld the steel.
Someone has to *build* the dream.

An artist makes a stunning plan,
a masterpiece from mind to hand:
a fountain, both unique and grand!

But . . .

Someone works to dig the trench,
lay the drains, solder seams.

Someone needs to plumb the pipes.
Someone has to *build* the dream.

A scientist earns a degree
in physics and ecology.
He aims toward cleaner energy.

But . . .

Someone works to tighten bolts,
steer the crane, drive machines.

Someone needs to raise the tower.
Someone has to *build* the dream.

Park designers sketch with pride
amusements and amazing rides
and sights to keep you mystified!

But . . .

Someone works to run the wires,
light the lights, make them gleam.

Someone needs to bury cables.
Someone has to *build* the dream.

An author thought up something new,

the illustrator planned and drew,
to make this book for kids like YOU!

But . . .

Someone worked to set the text,
run the press, load the reams.

Someone had to make THIS book!
Someone had to *build* this dream.

All across this great big world
there's lots of work to do.
It takes a *team* to build a dream,
a skilled, hard-working crew.

So when you see a bicycle,
a playground, house, or shoe,
remember all the *someones* who
helped make a dream come true.